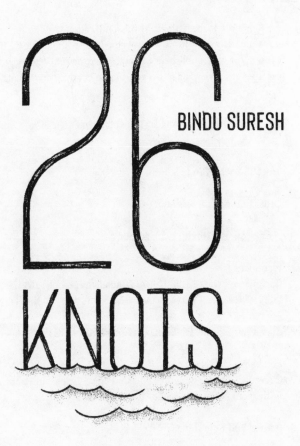

26 KNOTS

BINDU SURESH

Invisible Publishing
Halifax & Picton

Library and Archives Canada Cataloguing in Publication

Title: 26 knots / Bindu Suresh.

Other titles: Twenty-six knots

Names: Suresh, Bindu, 1983- author.

Identifiers:
Canadiana (print) 20190079673 | Canadiana (ebook) 20190079681
ISBN 9781988784243 (softcover) | ISBN 9781988784304 (HTML)

Classification: LCC PS8637.U754 A614 2019 | DDC C813/.6—dc23

Edited by Leigh Nash
Cover and interior design by Megan Fildes | Typeset in Laurentian
With thanks to type designer Rod McDonald

Printed and bound in Canada

Invisible Publishing | Halifax & Picton
www.invisiblepublishing.com

We acknowledge the support of the Canada Council for the Arts, which last year invested $20.1 million in writing and publishing throughout Canada.

Canada Council   Conseil des Arts
for the Arts   du Canada

ONTARIO ARTS COUNCIL
CONSEIL DES ARTS DE L'ONTARIO
an Ontario government agency
un organisme du gouvernement de l'Ontario

for Andrew Harder,
most honourable of men

I

Years later, he would reach out for her hand as she walked, oblivious, past where he was standing on the train paused at Lionel-Groulx. By then she will have drawn the nectar from every memory, dried the fallen petals with constant thought—the slightly ridiculous sway of his hips to jazz, the kisses in her creased palms as they made love, his crescent body arched around hers in the morning moonlight.

But then, on that warm June afternoon, that life was just beginning—Araceli and Adrien were simply two young journalists, their future before them like a field of long, swaying grass.

"This is my first fire," she had said, opening the slim spiral notebook to a blank page as they watched charred fragments of building chip from the facade, covering the ground before them like a slow and purposeful rain.

Adrien stood over his kitchen counter with a screwdriver, cracking open thick-shelled oysters and placing them in a glass bowl. Sébastien, a friend of Adrien's from the Gaspé who was staying with him for the summer, stood next to him, his leg outstretched to keep Adrien's black cat from jumping up onto the counter.

Araceli was looking at a photograph on the fridge. It had been cut in half, on an angle; it showed Adrien, his back against the ocean, his hair wet and tucked behind his ears. His right arm had been cut off at the shoulder, a perfect scissor-line caressing his cheek.

"I'd been at TVA for a year when the CBC called and offered me a job," Adrien said, his lips pursed as square fragments of shell fell into the sink. He gave a sheepish shrug. "So I said, well, yes, it's the CBC, so."

"So, you said yes," Araceli said, touching the edge of the photograph. "Is this the Gaspé?"

"It is," Adrien said. He paused, turning away slightly to wipe his wet hands on a dishtowel. "But come, I have better pictures."

In the living room he pulled out an album with dark blue covers. He put his arm around Araceli's waist as she flipped past seascapes, a picture of Adrien's sister against the Atlantic with a child in each arm. He placed his hand, shyly, on her leg.

"What do you think, Sébastien," he said, calling out toward the kitchen. "Isn't the Gaspé the most beautiful place in the world?"

He pressed his lips gently against her neck.

"Chez nous."

That night Adrien and Araceli made love for three hours. On the balcony under the moon and the swaying trees, in the humid summer air—her hands above her head and her fingers laced through his—he would stop to kiss her, still inside her.

Inside the bedroom, warm, his blond body curved around hers and their legs interwoven, because drying each other's skin with the rough purple towels had ended with her pushed against the tiled wall, his mouth on her throat, Araceli said, "I want to get to know you better."

Adrien laughed. Araceli nestled into his vocal cords as they rumbled against her forehead.

"What do you want to know?"

"I don't know," she said lightly, but thought: What did your face look like before? And the other day, when you were out on the stairs—were you crying? How do you behave around the people you do not love?

Adrien sat up and pulled Araceli onto his lap, folding his arms underneath her chest.

"It's just that we're so sex-centric. If we're left alone for five seconds we end up making love, wherever we are."

"That's what couples do when they're falling for each other," he said, kissing her on the cheek. "We have all summer to get to know each other."

Later that week, Araceli saw Adrien at a church in Notre-Dame-de-Grâce. They smiled at each other; they delighted in leaving his apartment each morning and not knowing if they would be thrown together again, sent to cover the same story at the same time.

The vestibule of the church was filled with long tables. Araceli crossed the room to meet Adrien; he stepped away from his cameraman. Looking at the family of refugees crowded at the table's end, he said, "That family from Bogotá. They've been here for a month and they're as attached to Montreal as if they'd been born here."

After the press conference, the three rejected refugees stood to one side, in the nave of the church, refusing to leave and void their claim to religious sanctuary. Araceli approached the mother, and then the daughter, neither of whom yet spoke much English or French; and, after she'd shared what she could remember of her time as a child in South America in their common language, they told her about the razors, the slashed arms, the skin wrapped in bloody newspaper. The woman called her husband over to show Araceli his scars.

Adrien sat next to her on the church's stone steps, his back against the pediment of a statue. This time he said, "I feel alone in Montreal. I feel like I don't belong here." He said the words evenly, as if by doing so he could reduce their weight.

Araceli smiled. She, who had moved from Argentina at the age of seven, who fell into a comfortable stride everywhere, who had watched her parents look at each other in wonderment, snapping their fingers, at the loss of simple words like mesa and cuchara.

To feel so lost after a move of only a few hundred kilometres: this was the sense of home, of having one's feet take root, that endeared Adrien to Araceli.

In English, Araceli was vibrant and cheerful; in Spanish, she was soft, maternal, with a voice from the undulating Córdoban hills; in French, she was endearingly wide-eyed and lost, tripping over her words as if they were large obstacles. Adrien liked her most, but knew her least, in his mother tongue.

II

The afternoon Pénélope met Gabriel at a high school cafeteria in Oka, he had been the only other adult there. Without a second thought, she had paid for her grilled cheese sandwich and taken the seat across from him.

"Let me guess," he said. "You were across the street and saw the sign."

Pénélope nodded. Gabriel folded his newspaper under his coffee cup.

"Believe it or not, we're actually lucky. That restaurant is terrible."

"You've been here before?"

"My mother works as a counsellor here," he explained. "I live in Montreal, so I try to visit her every once in a while. Where are you from?"

"Quebec City," Pénélope said. "But I live and work in Montreal. I'm a journalist. I'm doing a piece on Kanesatake—you know, something beyond arson, exile, and police blockades."

"I've never been to Quebec City," Gabriel replied. "Are you with the CBC?"

"No, TVA. I started there a year ago."

"TVA." Gabriel smiled. "Is that the building on de Maisonneuve, near Papineau? I think my firm might have built that."

An hour passed. The school bell had rung once, and then again; the cafeteria was now empty but for a handful of students.

"My sister Lille, I think, forgave our father more," she said. "She was younger. She saw much less of what he did to our mother."

"What did he do?"

"Nothing overt. He never hit her, for example. He just always made her feel unsafe, as if he were just about to leave. Or close their bank accounts."

"Are they still together?"

Pénélope paused. "No. My mother died a few years ago."

In the silence that followed, they heard the clattering of trays as the students at the table beside them got up to leave. Gabriel reached across the table and took Pénélope's hand in his own.

"I never knew my father," Gabriel said quietly. "I thought I did, but the man my mother said was my father turned out not to be. She kept the truth from me for years."

Only later, holding the double-striped pregnancy test up to the grey light of the bathroom window, or even after that, as she overlooked the rushing St. Lawrence from the Jacques Cartier Bridge, was Pénélope able to recognize this moment as a knot—as the first knot in an otherwise smooth life.

III

The woman in the photograph—the one whose cheek was pressed to Adrien's so tightly it had to be cut away—was Sinziana. Adrien remembered the first time he'd seen her, sitting directly in front of him in his third-year political theory seminar at Concordia. It was the first day of class, and from the fact that she was two seconds behind on every instruction given, Adrien realized she didn't speak English—it had been the same for him three years before, having moved from the Gaspé to attend university in Montreal.

He zipped up his backpack as quietly as possible. He kept his pencil and his notebook in hand as he stood, walked down his row of chairs, up hers, and sat down beside her. She had looked at him, grateful; only then did he realize that she was beautiful.

After class, he found out she was Romanian, and had just transferred from the Sorbonne. She had broken up with her boyfriend the month before, left her mother in Paris a year before that, and lost her father over a decade earlier in an anti-communist riot.

It was the first thing he liked about her. She forged ahead, alone, not the kind of girl who would doubt that you loved her, whose insecurity needled its way into every crevice, weakening the mortar of every wall.

Adrien came home from work—a father with a hunting rifle, first his wife holding her hands up over her face and their kids, screaming in circles, then all four of them dead, with interviews all day and his evening news report at six, in full view of the blood on the living room windows—to find his morning coffee cup sitting on top of a Bell phone bill. He lifted the mug to check the date.

"Sinziana?"

The wood floor creaked as she came into the kitchen, her arms covered in white paint and sawdust. She wiped her hands on a dishtowel, then placed it on the table next to the bill. "I thought you promised you wouldn't hide these from me anymore."

"I know. I'm sorry." Adrien reached over to cover Sinziana's paint-flecked fingers, his hands cold and stiff still from the December wind. "I just want you to be able to focus on your work. On creating something really beautiful."

"We talked about this already," she said, pulling her hands out from under his, picking up the coffee mug and taking it to the sink. "I'd rather worry about the phone bill than feel like I don't live here. You don't share anything with me."

Sinziana tossed the coffee mug onto the dirty dishes; they heard two or three of them break. She glanced at Adrien. She saw the corners of his mouth tighten briefly. He was still looking down, now at the Hydro-Québec invoice stacked under the phone bill.

"It's just I..." she started. Her voice wavered. She looked into the sink, her eyes full of tears; the edges of that morning's cups and bowls were blurry. "You would never have done this with Stéphanie."

"I didn't even live with Stéphanie."

Sinziana fingered the edge of a broken plate. It had split very evenly in half. She hated the way he was looking at her now—calmly, as if she were an illogical child.

Adrien stood and walked into the next room; Sinziana heard him sit down and roll the chair toward the desk. A few seconds later she heard the scattered tapping of his father's typewriter.

She paused, then pulled up a breakfast plate from the sink and, using two purposeful hands, slammed it against the floor. She watched as the triangular shards of broken china flew as far as the table legs and slid under the fridge. The cereal bowl, smashed next, broke into four curved fragments, covering the kitchen floor with nuts and milk.

Adrien came out of his study and watched her. A piece of china rested near one of his toes. Sinziana, watching him, dropped every dish from the sink, then every clean dish in the cupboard, methodically working through the saucers, wineglasses, and serving platters. She avoided anything she knew wouldn't break.

Half-asleep, Adrien lifted his head and looked down toward the foot of the bed. The skin of his calves felt wet and sticky against the bedsheets. He sat up quickly, tearing off the blankets, lifting his leg from the blood-soaked silk. Sinziana, lying next to him, was breathing rapidly; her skin was pallid and tears darkened her thick eyelashes. Adrien placed his hand gently on her stomach.

"I could feel it bleeding away," she choked, turning her face toward him.

"You should have woken me up," he said, his hand still on her pale, flat stomach as it rose and fell. "Does it hurt?" Sinziana shook her head. Adrien looked down at the red delta spread between her legs, all the way past his knees. He felt his chest tighten between his shoulder blades, as if his body were being crushed inward.

Her legs began to shake.

"We'll get you to the hospital," he said. "Right away."

Adrien wiped Sinziana's clammy, trembling skin with a soft cloth, made her coffee and toast she couldn't swallow, and helped her get dressed, like a little girl, in loose pyjama bottoms and an old T-shirt. He helped her scared eyes into the taxi cab and sat in the hospital waiting room with her until they were called in.

The next night he watched her sleep, sweat-soaked despite the mid-winter chill, while he sat on the edge of the bed, wakeful and restless.

And then, after three days of gazing out into the out-of-focus world, of tripping over their steps, they awoke in each other's arms, cold, with veils hanging over their faces—under shrouds that let them hide from each other.

Sinziana's last night in the apartment on des Érables—the one that prompted the scissors, the careful separation of faces in the pale light of a grey dawn—was on a cold March evening, after she discovered the ashes of two different brands of cigarettes.

"I found this today," she had said, placing the black ashtray in front of Adrien.

"I don't get it."

"Two different cigarettes, Adrien. Two. Who was over here? Did you think I wouldn't find this?"

Adrien sat back in his chair. Outside, rain poured down the tightened windows and froze, droplet over droplet, keeping the warm glow of the candlelight inside.

"This is ridiculous, you know."

Sinziana cocked her head.

"Marie-Ève is an old friend from Chicoutimi. She came over this afternoon for coffee. She wanted to meet you, actually," Adrien said. "If you had come home earlier, you two could have met."

"I'm sure that's exactly what you would have wanted." Sinziana walked into her studio, where she lifted the creaking lid of her pottery kiln with two mitts, her face reddening from the steam and heat. She turned to face him, looking back through the candlelit doorway. "You could live perfectly well without me, couldn't you?"

Adrien held up his hands and pushed his chair back. "This is ridiculous," he said again, standing up.

Sinziana fumbled through the noisy tool box on the work table. She was searching for something to busy her hands, desperately stalling while she looked for a way to pull herself back over the precipice she had thought to be rescued from.

What she had wanted: *Of course not, sweetheart. If you leave, every love I have after you will be but a bridge I build over an abyss.* Or: *Sinziana, if you left this place I would come to loathe it, for bearing your footprints without holding your weight.*

It was then, seeking above all to bring him back to her as he strode away, that Sinziana grasped the old wooden handle with its two rusted rivets; that she felt the bright silver knife fall into her hands, even as home—the home with the stencilled flowers she had drawn on the walls and the man she had slept quietly against—slipped out of them.

They stood as if in a duel. Adrien watched Sinziana, who was breathing quickly, drops of sweat on her forehead and nose. He saw the sharp point in her loose grip. From the darkness of the kitchen he looked at her, arrogant, knowing he could now blame her as he broke it off.

IV

Gabriel remembered sitting in the kitchen with his mother, near the oven, her baking an apple pie, and then a cherry pie, both burned around the edges to a deep brown crisp. She placed a warm, damp palm on his knee. She had tears in the corners of her eyes as she told him, again, about the plane crash, about his father: his flying thousands of metres above cold rocks and summer lakes, and then his fumbling hands on the controls and the static on the radio, the quiet downward glide between the trees. He died, she said, not in the belly-first collision that had killed those standing, but after, later, in the final gas-lit explosion that incinerated them all.

She had pictures of Gabriel, as a five-year-old, at his father's funeral. He had held the ashes, she said, the mixture of soot and body and airplane, the singed dirt.

But there was one detail his mother had overlooked: that in a town of fifty thousand, a bogus, fabricated plane crash was even harder to substantiate than a bogus, fabricated father. She had underestimated, too, how certain clues would reveal the truth to her son—the shared private glances of other parents; the teachers who were a little too kind; the unabashed, pointed laughter of other children—so that by the time Gabriel was fourteen, he knew that parts of her story were too well-written, and that others gaped, empty as an animal's yawning jaws.

V

Adrien brought the cigarette to his lips, the embered tip glowing against the dark trees and hidden rooftops of the Plateau. The unvarnished wood of the balcony was soaked with rainwater; on it sat Adrien, naked, and Araceli, her legs still wrapped around his waist, her shoulders covered with a blanket.

"Adrien," Araceli said. "How did your last relationship end?"

Adrien told her about Sinziana and the ectopic pregnancy. In the darkness, Araceli smiled at his soft accent, at the shorter *o*, the quicker *y*; at the same time she felt a heavy weight sink into her chest, imagining him having to translate those words, explain them over and over again.

"I don't think either of us recovered from losing the baby. At least, not enough to stay together."

"I'm so sorry that happened."

"It's okay. It wasn't meant to be. I had always been very excited about having kids, but somehow I wasn't with her. Not near the end."

Adrien put out his cigarette against the wood floor of the balcony, tightening his arms around Araceli's waist.

"She was very difficult to live with," he said. "One day, we'd gotten into a fight. She asked me to meet her later that night after work at a bar on Crescent. When I got there, she was dressed up, toute belle, and she just sat there. She wouldn't even look at me. She ignored me all night."

It started to rain again. Adrien cupped his hand against the small of Araceli's back, making a pool of the rivulet of rainwater that flowed down her spine. "What about your last relationship?"

"We fought a lot," Araceli said. "Every day, every hour, over whether or not I really loved him. Then, one night, he said he knew I loved him but that he was sure he loved me more. And he was right. That was it. And it was over, even though we stayed together for a year after that." The sharp, cold rain stung Araceli's exposed calves. "I will never do that again," she said. "Be the one who loves less."

Together, Adrien and Araceli had, at the most, a couple of months—and three weeks of these Adrien had spent in the Gaspé without her, leaving Montreal on his motorcycle to drive twelve hours up the long, jagged coast.

"Remember what you are worth," his father had said the last time, when he'd announced to his family that Sinziana was pregnant. She, that night, had sat in the corner, on the oversized brown chesterfield: shy, swallowed by cushions, lost for words.

This time, about Araceli, the old man had said, walking with his middle child beside the grey waves, stepping slowly along the rocky, cold beach: "I don't see it in your eyes this time. I don't."

When Adrien returned to Montreal, his legs stiff from the journey, his fingertips cold beneath his gloves, he had forgotten Sinziana. And he might have chosen Araceli, even against his father's advice, had it not been for Pénélope.

Araceli had ordered breakfast, and then lunch; outside the café on Saint Catherine, rain plastered pictures of naked dancers to the sidewalk. Adrien had not called, not since yesterday, when, gruff and recently awoken, he had promised that today he would take her to explore Trois-Rivières.

And now, alone at the table, her two unfinished meals waiting beside her unblinking phone, she felt as if she were galloping through a prairie field with the reins cut, as if she had stepped off a shelf into an ocean of limitless depth.

Between Sinziana and Pénélope, Araceli had no chance; the past and the future were equally heavy burdens that limited the present to a sliver, a small crack in a doorway. She was the path between two destinations, a body to lie and stretch across like the wild terrain between cities, between homes; someone Adrien loved because she pulled him through the eye of a needle, brought him to the gentle stroke of his thumb against his fiancée's forehead, to her large white breasts falling against each other like soft mountains in the pale moonlight.

That August, one week after Adrien had met Pénélope, Adrien and Araceli came to the same instantaneous, silent conclusion: that Araceli, carrying two awkward suitcases up the precipitous outdoor staircase, had hardly anything in the apartment to pack.

There were no photographs to cut in half. There were no bloody bedsheets to throw out, no cords of kinship to be prematurely severed. She had a toothbrush, a hair dryer, a sweater from their first date, maybe, but nothing of a weight that had to be borne, packed away, or buried in storage. She had underlined exactly one paragraph in one book, in pencil. And even now, after three months, she walked cautiously around the apartment, turning on unfamiliar lights in the unfamiliar dark, creeping with the gait of a guest, with a stranger's quiet footsteps.

All this to say: it was comparatively easy for Adrien to feel like he had erased Araceli, a fact, of course, that made it nearly impossible for Araceli to do the same.

But what Adrien discovered, after Araceli left on a one-way ticket to New York City: that a connection cut short was impossible to forget; that love, when skipped over, rests as a pebble lodged in one's memory.

VI

For Adrien, the loss of Araceli coincided with the departure of his best friend, Sébastien, who moved his few belongings out of Adrien's apartment the day after Araceli left. Sébastien had been waiting in the kitchen that last night, as Adrien broke the news to Araceli in the doorway, and then insisted on taking her out for dinner as planned; he had been there when they returned; he had sat next to Adrien on the windowsill later that night, listening to Araceli play the piano. There to add an air of camaraderie, of normalcy, to the desertion.

Sébastien had done so stony-faced: he, who had paid particular attention not to prepare food with milk or wheat; who had listened, the door ajar, to Adrien making love to Araceli on the balcony; who, within a few weeks of knowing her, had made grandiose statements he actually meant, that she was always welcome at his family's home in the Gaspé, and that he loved her, already, like a sister or a friend.

"My friend, tu t'es fait emporter par une vieille fille," Sébastien said after he met Pénélope. After this, Adrien ignored his calls.

Among the August losses from the apartment on des Érables: one ash-coloured, rolled-up mattress; a guitar case and sheet music; an old friend's squash racquet and indoor court shoes.

VII

Pénélope knew that, by now, Adrien would be back at the apartment waiting for her. They had left his place at six that morning, Adrien dressed in polyester gym shorts that hung down to his knees, a scuffed white volleyball in hand, Pénélope wearing the black patent heels and black-and-white checkered dress she'd had on the day before.

Adrien had been flustered, so invested was he in her errand. Still, he knew better than to sit at home, his whole body trembling, while his rival lifted his fingertips to her lips, whispering the old, soft endearments. While the minutes for her were hours, those same minutes were, for Adrien, days.

It had taken eight hours, but she had done it; six hours to and from Quebec City, and two more to move her ex from kissing her cheekbones to the other side of his bedroom, where he pulled open drawers and threw underwear, socks, blouses—even things that weren't hers. He tore pants and dresses from their hangers in the closet that, in the particularly brutal and practical manner of those who have fallen out of love, she picked up and stuffed into her bag. It saved her having to come back.

Adrien greeted her with relief. He had been afraid, secretly, that she wouldn't really do it.

He rented a cottage, by the sea—not far from his parents' house in the Gaspé—and took her there on a five-day weekend that saw them each call in sick. When they returned, he started driving to Quebec City every other day, after work; he had to leave Pénélope's bed before sunrise to make it back to Montreal in time to deliver the early-morning news.

Pénélope made the same trip in reverse, and after a few sleep-deprived weeks, Adrien watched her close her eyes, for a full two or three seconds, in the middle of a televised interview with the leader of the opposition.

In their first month together, Adrien studied his new girlfriend's deep-set eyes, the long bridge of her nose, her naturally mauve lips. He watched her move, back and forth, from the balcony to the bed. He started to use words like *we*, *us*, *our*; he'd even let slip the phrases *your shelf, your drawer*.

Three months later, when Pénélope took a pay cut and a demotion to move to Montreal and work for TVA—to be near him—Adrien walked down to Phillips Square and bought a ring with clusters of diamonds and swirls of white gold, which he hid in the bedroom closet behind his old political science notes.

VIII

The night Adrien broke up with her, Araceli had taken the steep, badly lit steps up to his apartment slowly, though he was waiting at the head of the stairs, a blond giant, and she could feel his eyes and mouth embracing her already. She laughed up at him as she held her skirt above her knees.

Adrien's breath was soft on her neck. Her fingers were wrapped in his hair. He murmured, she murmured back. His arms draped loosely around her torso. She pressed her lips to his, but he stood solid, resisting her; his head was a marble bust. She kissed him again, touching the sides of his face, and his lips held firm, firm in the decision they'd made. By the third kiss, his lips were patiently limp.

"I have something to tell you," he said.

Standing there, on the threshold at the top of the stairs, Adrien told her he loved someone else. And, when he told her about the weekend beach-house rental he had arranged for himself and his new girlfriend, in the Gaspé—when Araceli learned that he, too, was capable of such a commitment, of lunging after the months of aimless parries, with her—she felt love slide through her like a spear of light, like an arrow, as pure and white as moonlight.

What had happened: Adrien went to meet a fellow Radio-Canada journalist from Quebec City—a sidewalk-corner meeting arranged by text message between live hits—and felt dizzy the moment he saw her on Marie-Anne. He blacked out, and when he woke he was lying on the ground with her lips against his.

Araceli took a step down one stair. The years of lying to him began: first, here, with her eyes and her body, seeming to take the news in stride. Then, two years later, meeting him on a wintry street corner, with the kisses on each cheek, her joy at hearing of his engagement. And, monthly, every time she called him or he called her, with the ease in her voice that was the ultimate lie: that she could bear to just be his friend.

Lies of such immensity they surpassed their love in memory, for him as well as her.

If there was a consolation prize, Araceli had won it. Finally, they descended the stairs, together. He consoled her on the wet sidewalk on the way to their favourite pizzeria, her hand clasped to his chest in friendship.

"You are my friend, and I care about you," Adrien said, stumbling over *friend* as if ashamed to say it, as if surprised at the word.

Araceli, for the first time, heard Pénélope's name—asked for it, in fact—then asked where Pénélope lived, what she was like, when he'd realized he loved her.

"It was like a flash of lightning," he said. Le coup de foudre.

"You are my friend," Adrien repeated, skirting over the word as a flat pebble skips across a cold mountain lake, a sliver slipping through skin.

Over dinner, he explained everything. He had been seventeen the first time he had made love, with Stéphanie, his first girlfriend. The first time he'd had sex was before that, when he was fifteen, with a girl he had just met at a campfire on a Gaspé beach. Making love and having sex, after all, were two different things.

"Don't you agree?" he asked from across the table.

And Araceli, who had only ever made love, who years later, in the arms of a half-dozen other men, would still only be making love to him, of course, agreed.

IX

That afternoon in Oka, Pénélope and Gabriel sat with their palms flat on the low tables, her dark hair reflecting the afternoon's late light, his laugh, deep and rumbling, starting in his chest and moving up through his shoulders and hands—until the last school bells had rung and the hallway fell empty and silent. They had spoken for long enough that Gabriel knew, as they walked down the crumbling concrete steps, as he strode over the sparse yellow grass with her slim fingers woven between his large ones, that she was taken by someone else, that there was a shared apartment together in the Plateau. Still, he pulled her through the crisp fall air; still, he pulled her toward the trees and the sunset. And Pénélope, though she remembered Adrien's clear blue eyes behind hers in the mirror, though she said his name to herself and felt the full blood push through her veins—still her fingers clung urgently, still she followed, skipping to keep up with Gabriel's faster stride.

It was six and already it was completely dark. A cold wind rustled the dry, crisp leaves still on their branches. Gabriel and Pénélope crackled over small forest twigs, crushing fallen pine cones under their hasty, scrambling feet.

They stopped in a glade. Pénélope rested her back against the trunk of an elm; Gabriel pressed his thumb and forefinger against her cheekbones. He stroked her neck, the base of her throat, the small triangle of skin exposed by her jacket. His hands were gentle, awed, and a bit surprised still, as if he, too, had been pulled through the trees.

Beneath this, Pénélope felt the rough insistence of his fingertips, the pressure of his torso against hers, and pulled him inside her, her hands gripping his back.

Then his breath against her neck, against the tree, the northern wind caressing the naked bark.

Pénélope stayed in the musty, darkened cabin—room number four at Oka's only hotel—for a week, waiting for the wounds to heal.

During the day, when Gabriel was out with his mother, Pénélope lay naked under the ceiling fan in the unseasonal October heat, daydreaming. She remembered the evening, three days ago now, that Gabriel had first made love to her. She had undone the buttons of her blouse hurriedly, nearly tearing them loose from the cloth, naked from the waist up, the weight of Gabriel's body pressing her back against the tree. The rough bark of late autumn had scraped her skin until she was raw and bleeding.

For six days she trailed her fingers over her torn shoulders—
for six days she turned cuts into scars so small that Adrien
would never see them, so large that he would never again
touch the skin underneath.

In the cooler nights, Gabriel told Pénélope about his youth, and about his mother, Rachel:

"When I was eighteen, I left home," he said. "I had two months of high school left but it didn't matter. I went to Kingston to live with my uncle, Jacob. I confronted my mother about the story of the plane crash and she told me that the pilot was a family friend, not my father. And that my father was still alive.

"When I got to Kingston, my uncle told me what he knew: how his father had stalked the entrance hall in front of the heavy oak door he had locked against Rachel, muttering that his daughter was a Jezebel, a harlot. Rachel screamed outside for hours, long after their parents had gone upstairs, while their five other siblings crowded onto the landing, listening to Rachel yell that her clothes had been torn off, that she had been raped.

"It was the first time I heard the word spoken out loud," he said. "The next day, my mother left on the early-morning bus to North Bay. One of her brothers went down to the penitentiary with a wooden baseball bat to find Marcel Tremblay, but he was gone already, too.

"And I thought, right then," Gabriel said, "is it enough that I now know who my father is, or do I need him to recognize my face, and admit what he did to my mother, before I kill him?"

X

The second time Pénélope kissed Adrien—after their first dinner date, a few hours after he had come to on the sidewalk, in her arms—she had pressed her hand against his chest, flat-palmed, her lips moving toward him even as her body seemed to push him away.

Later, Adrien came to see that these oft-conflicting signals were a pervasive feature of life with her. It was like having to learn a totally new language: a missed call from her aunt was always returned the same day, even though this aunt had been the scourge of her childhood; she only bought guidebooks for places she never intended to visit; she had a friend, Amélie, who, from the pressed childhood letters slid between the pages of Pénélope's high school yearbooks, had seemed to be her closest, her dearest, even though Pénélope rarely spoke about her.

It was a translation that, after a few months, he began to make automatically; a skill that, in a way, made him totally unfit to love anybody else.

XI

"It's at Saint Laurent and René Lévesque," Gabriel said.

"That's right downtown."

"But nobody will be there," Gabriel pointed out. "Construction holiday, remember?"

"I think you're taking the name a bit too literally."

Gabriel paused.

"You're mad about yesterday."

"Having no father is better than a bad father," Gabriel had said, the flat of his foot resting against a granite block, his fingers tracing the tan lines under her left breast. Pénélope lay against a fleece blanket, the bones of her lower back bruised from their hard bed of newly dried concrete.

"Well, what you said wasn't fair. He was a bad husband, not a bad father. They're not the same thing," Pénélope said. "Anyway, I'll call you later. I'm almost at work."

Another pause. "Please come today."

Gabriel knew that he should already be on the train, heading toward Montmorency. Yet, since falling in love with Pénélope, he had lost all scale, all measure, and he now treasured these moments alone in the firm's Mile End office, spent measuring the arc of a balcony down to a millimetre, conforming to the straight lead line of the ruler.

All this because the daily arithmetic of life with her provided no right answers. What did it mean that Pénélope had kissed his nose and not his lips? That she had made him wait an hour for her, alone at dinner—paranoid that she'd left him, paranoid that Adrien had found out, lost his temper, and hurt her in some way—because to call would have been suspicious?

How was he supposed to know what a single action meant, if a kiss was both *this is a lie and I love someone else* and *you are the only one for me*?

It was past eight when Gabriel left his office. Walking down Saint Laurent, he took a sharp left on Laurier, striding down into the metro station and taking the orange line in the wrong direction. He conformed to this, too, another of Pénélope's panicked demands—that, leaving the offices of his architectural firm on Saint Viateur and Clark, he take the metro northwest first, before crossing the platform and heading downtown to the Old Port to meet her.

Some days, he recognized that if they were caught, it would be unexpected: they would be on Crescent, laughing, happy, their fingertips brushing in lieu of holding hands, sauntering down the street as Adrien walked up it; or that Pénélope would misread Adrien's schedule again, confusing the sixteenth for the fifteenth, and they would be making love in the apartment she shared with Adrien at precisely the moment he had been in a conference the day before. It was unrealistic, Gabriel knew, to think that Adrien would be sitting across from him in the same metro car, would know who he was, and would deduce the illicit nature of a direct Laurier-to-Square-Victoria trajectory.

On most days, though, Gabriel kept an eye over his shoulder, having swallowed Pénélope's terror at being caught whole; he screened numbers he didn't recognize, and started to carry a small pocket knife, as if he were the one who should fear, he the one who had been wronged.

They had just finished making love on Adrien's couch. Gabriel held his weight on his forearms, on either side of Pénélope's chest. She was breathing quietly now, with one leg bent against the stiff back of the sofa and the other stretched out, dangling over the edge. Gabriel kissed her collarbone, lifted himself up, and walked to the bathroom.

When he came back, Pénélope was on her hands and knees, searching the crevices of the couch with scrambling fingers, as if she were blind. The sofa pillows were strewn around the living room. In a pile in the middle of the sofa frame he noticed bent paper clips, safety pins, a dead battery, the reddish-gold bobby pins she used. She stood to face him, her hair still wild from their lovemaking.

"I'm sorry, it's just that Adrien and I haven't had sex on this couch for a while," she said breathlessly, a half-dozen of the pins in her outstretched hand.

For the first time, Gabriel wasn't angry, didn't mind that she'd substituted *had sex* for *made love* or that she'd used that voice, again—the tentative voice that emerged whenever she was forced to allude to her relationship with Adrien. Instead, he saw for the first time what her life had become, plunged in the murky water of constant deception—and, for a brief second, thought less of her.

And so he told her, firmly, naturally, and easily this time, that she had to choose—knowing she had to do so before his new-found pity shrunk her so completely there was nothing left to love.

What Pénélope grew to hate, during the course of her affair: realizing Adrien was home when she didn't think he would be, his sudden hand on her shoulder, the apartment dark; surprises of any kind; or any of Adrien's small loyalties, like the answering-machine message from his ex-girlfriend Stéphanie he had listened to and then immediately deleted, without even knowing Pénélope was in the next room.

She also resented that everything new and beautiful had to be hidden: that, lying quietly in the darkness, Adrien panting desperately on top of her, it was impossible for her to suggest the position she and Gabriel had discovered— her legs spread out like the petals of a lotus and her ankles anchored down—that would bring her to orgasm within seconds; that, in the mornings now, she turned away from Adrien to get dressed, toward the window, slipping on an opaque bra that hid the tanned skin around her large nipples, bronzed from the afternoons of making love between the unfinished walls of half-built homes.

She hated Adrien's face when they had sex—he with his eyes fully open, the disquieting frankness of his surrender.

It was a drowsy, near-silent afternoon. The rich yellow sunlight fell onto the bare wood of the balcony. "I need to read inside," she said, one leg dangling over the other. "I'm going to suffocate out here."

The apartment was dark and musty. Pénélope walked over to the bookshelf and placed the novel she'd been reading, open and spine up, on top of a row of books. She took out another one; its blue jacket was faded and worn, almost white, and she had to flip through the first few pages to find a legible title: *The Sound and the Fury*. As she thumbed through the rest of the book, a twice-folded piece of paper, torn from a notebook and yellowed, fell out from between the pages. On it, Pénélope read, *A woman, a love, that changes with the seasons*? and a series of scrawled notes in Adrien's hand.

Then she noticed the two hearts in the margin, *Pénélope et Adrien*, and *Adrien et Pénélope*, and for a second saw his love as he saw it—and knew she couldn't do as Gabriel had asked.

XII

The realization, when it arrived, was swift as an executioner's blade. Adrien had said, when Araceli called from New York, the phone cradled between his shoulder and his ear: "My life has never been better." These six words—and her discovery that he could, indeed, live without her—severed Araceli's life in two.

XIII

After sharing the story of how Gabriel's mother had fled Kingston, Jacob warned Gabriel that he was going to call her and let her know Gabriel was safe.

Gabriel assented with relief; he had already called home as soon as he'd hit Pembroke, and explained to her, even-toned, that he'd left, that he was too far away to follow, that he wasn't coming back. He listened to her sob in gasps. He was shocked that he had managed to reach her at all; in his entire life, his mother had never taken a single day off of work. He had mumbled a few inanities: I promise to finish school this year, wherever I end up, I'll get a job, I'll be fine. His voice had wavered then and he'd hung up—and he'd wanted to hitchhike, steal, borrow a car, do anything, to get back to her.

But Gabriel had another half, a half he understood better now, his father's half that constantly battled with his mother's—fighting, thrashing, kicking—and that day it was his father's half that won as Gabriel stood red-eyed, waiting to reboard the bus toward Kingston.

Gabriel enrolled at Bayridge Secondary School, not far fromwhere Jacob lived on Princess Street. He couldn't believe that, in the time it had taken to move from one city to another, from one life into the next—in the time it had taken to call his mother's bluff, discover that his father had been a prison guard, not a dead pilot, and, armed with the truth, feel suddenly sure-footed—he had only missed one full day of classes. It was as if he had been in outer space, for years, only to return to earth and find that only a few seconds had elapsed.

In his years away from North Bay, Gabriel didn't learn much more about his father. From Jacob, he learned that the man had been brilliant, a womanizer, violent. To his first-year roommate, a criminology major who'd needed to draw a police sketch for an assignment, he'd given the only other information he knew: that his father was a white male, likely in his mid-forties, of average height, broad-shouldered, French-Canadian. Gabriel had carried this poorly drawn rendition around for weeks, eyeing the vaguely handsome face.

And so far, he had only told Caroline, his first girlfriend. Or half-told her. They had been in a fight, and he had said, "Come on, by now you must have figured out how I was born," afraid she would no longer want him, seeing how he saw his own life as an abomination. But she had simply seemed confused. And then, when she realized what he meant, she gave him a kind of helpless *that's all?* look before she said, "Well, my mother wanted an abortion. Just because they didn't want us to exist, it doesn't mean we shouldn't." She went on, but his affection for her deepened—for that look she'd given him, which couldn't conceive of his shame.

With that confession, Gabriel had felt an enormous relief. He had been struggling upward, against the weight of fathoms of dark water, trying to be happy for three people: for his mother, to make up for the solitude his birth had reinforced; for himself; and to spite his father, always to spite his father. Now he realized: Someone else knows, and I am no less existent. And: I am no more imprisoned by who my parents are than is any other human on earth.

And so the next time his mother called, Gabriel—who had managed for most of his university years to keep in touch with his mother through letters—actually answered, and made plans to go to North Bay to see her.

XIV

Under the table, Gabriel's outstretched leg rested against Pénélope's calf. Fall-red maples cast windblown shadows over his face. Not looking at her, he asked: "When are you going to tell him?"

"Soon."

"You said soon a year ago. You said soon the first day we met."

"I just need a few more weeks," she said. "He just asked me to marry him. I don't want to be cruel."

"I can't believe you said yes," he said. "That would have been the time, if you were ever really planning on breaking up with him."

"That's not fair," she said. "This is easy for you."

"I don't see that it is." Pénélope felt the muscles in his legs tighten. "It's not easy being in love with someone who's fucking somebody else."

They were at a bar in Côte-des-Neiges, on the terrasse, far from work, far from their homes—one balconied and wood-floored with a sleeping man inside, the other a mostly empty studio with a rooftop terrace near Atwater—so far from the familiar streets where they practised their deceptions that each felt a bit lost, even from the other.

But really, why the delay?

A week earlier, on a crisp September morning two weeks into a late period, Pénélope realized that another type of knot— the kind that doubled, and then tripled over itself, the kind with the power to tie her to one man or the other forever— had woven itself into the thin thread of her life.

How could she reconcile that this nascent love was completely unrelated to the identity of the father, but that her entire happiness depended on who the father was?

Pénélope felt like she was stabbing Adrien in the face with a white dagger. Worse, that she had sidled in, a leg between his legs, her tongue between his lips; she had tilted her breasts against his chest and felt his nipples harden, and as he moaned, she swept the cotton swab from the corner of his mouth over his lower lip.

It had been worse, earlier that night, with Gabriel. Her knees straddling his hips, he fast asleep and open-mouthed beneath her, she had agreed with him suddenly; she felt ashamed of her two bedrooms, her two lingerie drawers, of having excited two men in one night.

Later, Pénélope stood by the window, naked, the night mist gathered in droplets on the cold glass. She stepped onto the balcony, a blanket over her shoulders—unable to slide back into bed with Adrien, afraid of finding a real wound in his flesh.

The moist Q-tip in a plastic bag labelled A, next to the one labelled G.

Adrien stepped out into a cloudy Tuesday morning, his motorcycle helmet in hand. There was a mist in the air that dampened his skin as he followed the cat down the steps to the sidewalk. In the gutter, rainwater surged past like a muddy river.

Swinging a leg over the seat, the weight of his left foot pressed into the footrest, Adrien noticed the garbage bags Pénélope had taken out the night before. They had been clawed and knocked over by raccoons; a trail of trash led into the gutter and flowed down the street with twists of yellow leaves. Near the edge of the sidewalk, he saw the fateful plastic tip, the white casing partly obscured by a damp fold of newspaper, and the screen with the two blue lines.

Wiping the pregnancy test against his grey pants, he pulled the garbage bag upright, knotted the handles, and headed back inside.

Adrien arrived breathless. Pénélope was still asleep on the balcony, her white blanket moist with dew and drawn around her body. He squeezed her arm, gently, until she awoke.

"Nélo, were you waiting to tell me?" he asked.

"I wanted it to be a surprise," she murmured, still half-asleep, as he slid his arms under her thighs and her shoulders and carried her inside.

When Pénélope awoke, the first thing she saw on the bedside table was the pregnancy test she had thrown away herself, late yesterday night, the rest of the garbage clutched in her left fist as a decoy. How had Adrien found it?

She heard the slow press of his weight against the creaking floorboards. He slid into bed beside her, stroking her stomach and resting one arm between her breasts.

"Shouldn't you be on your way to work?" Pénélope asked as lightly as possible, her face turning away from his, her cheeks reddening.

"I found something incredible on the street today," he said, kissing her collarbone, and then her neck. "I can't believe you didn't explode from wanting to tell me."

"I was going to tell you tomorrow."

Adrien turned her body toward his.

"Nélo," he said, smiling broadly, the flat of his palm against her cheek.

She'd been drowsy and defenceless. Her prepared lies—
it's a friend's test, it must be the neighbour's garbage—
had evaporated, unwittingly leaving her with the best lie
of all, the prerogative of the hopeful mother: I wanted it
to be a surprise.

After dropping the two swabs off at the clinic where her sister's best friend worked, Pénélope returned to the apartment on des Érables to a fridge filled with her favourite foods—to strawberries and cream, chocolate, frozen yogourt—and to six tender, whispered messages on the answering machine, like the ones she and Adrien had traded in the first month after they'd met. And then, when Adrien came home from work, the devotion in his eyes with such finality.

Pénélope thought of her mother, the stacks of rubber-band-bound twenty-dollar bills stuffed into a purse in her closet—in case the shared accounts were drained, in case she needed to leave suddenly with her daughters. She remembered the scattered evidence of her father's other women, obvious even to her as a child.

Guilt sat on her shoulders like a boulder. Because she knew she'd been a coward, that she had, until now, prized being locked up safe in Adrien's guileless arms over her love for Gabriel, rough and unhewn, whole but slippery in her hands.

XV

Araceli finally returned to visit Montreal—a city she loved before she knew Adrien in it, as if she could tell in advance that only these acres of land would bring her happiness—to conduct interviews for the *New York Times*.

She stepped out of the airport into the sun and the chilly air of late autumn, walking toward a line of cabs. She thought, briefly, that she wouldn't call him, but from the moment she landed, Adrien was everywhere: his sock-clad feet padded the wooden floors of his living room, and Araceli heard his footfalls echo behind her; he took a deep breath on his balcony, and she felt the warmth of his exhale on the back of her neck.

In the taxi, on her way into the city, she texted him. And Adrien texted her back, immediately, with a time and place for lunch the next day.

Araceli saw Adrien in everyone. First, in the blond curls of a young girl holding her father's hand in line at a bakery, her hair settled on the nape of her neck just as Adrien's did. Then, seen from behind, a man near an indoor pool, his legs spread apart, his hips pushed forward slightly, as Adrien's would be, like him a small triangle of hair on his lower back. Then, near a library, a young man with Adrien's face, with exactly his face.

And then Adrien himself, walking down the north side of de Maisonneuve three years after they last parted, Araceli on an early-morning plane toward Manhattan, nearly missed; there he was, with those ridiculous glasses and unshaven face and oh, that beauty, and Araceli realized that there was nothing of those other three in him.

They walked down Saint Laurent and into a restaurant in Chinatown, moving to chairs sheltered from the November wind; scarved and gloved couples flanked them on either side. Adrien insisted on paying for lunch. And at the end, just as their plates were being cleared, he said, "I'm going to be a father soon."

Araceli thought: The last three years have been thin as a dying breath, as a winter wind over naked fields; the three summer months I was with you were as thick and heavy as blood fighting to course a broken body. It has been three years already, for your love for Pénélope to grow, for a child to grow inside her, and my love for you has not aged a day.

XVI

Pénélope picked up the phone. Adrien had been about to say, *This whole day, it's been like flying*, when the hoarseness of her voice drew him back to the triangle of blood on the bedsheets, the early-morning emergency-room visit: "Something's wrong," she said. "I have to talk to you when you get home."

Adrien took a taxi. He didn't trust himself to drive his motorcycle; already he felt the cold seep of autumn in his fingers and toes, felt fear curl like a fallen leaf around his heart.

"The baby is fine," Pénélope reassured when he arrived, reaching for his fingers like a sympathetic hostess.

When she spoke again, it was of the small cabin where she had stayed with another man. She spoke of the trees outside the window, the leaves crisp and rigid against their stalks, the cold greyness of the sky. "Everything else was dying and I was not," Pénélope said.

"His name, I want his *name*," Adrien heard himself say.

"It was the most intense connection I'd ever felt," she said.

Only then did he notice the two brown suitcases. So this had been arranged in advance—was her lover picking her up at a certain time? How many minutes would she oblige their years together? He felt like a fool, he who had thought to know everything she thought.

"What I ask myself," Adrien said, as if giving a speech, "is why a man would seduce a woman who was with somebody else, who was having a baby with somebody else."

Pénélope blinked quickly, her left hand protecting her stomach, stepping backwards as if he might hurt her. When had she become such an actress? Was she doing it on purpose, to add insult to injury? So that she could, in the end, blame him? For a second, faced with her feigned terror of him, it was as if he didn't know her, and his sudden hatred swept him blind.

"His name is Gabriel," she said finally, a suitcase in each hand, knowing he hadn't really wanted to hear it.

XVII

Adrien felt as if there were an abyss around every corner—nearly anything could remind him of Pénélope and her infidelity. Today it had been a white piece of printer paper, loosely affixed to the wall of the doctor's office with Scotch tape: "Get paid participation in our study—for couples who have started a new sexual relationship in the last two years."

He ran errands. He greased the joints of the bedroom door. He replaced the missing wheel on the dishwasher rack. He bought the cat four different kinds of cat food. He tidied the apartment, and then allowed his belongings to become scattered around it again.

Adrien doubled back, paced around city blocks in circles, crossed to walk down the other side of the same street. He thought: Was I wrong? Was the feeling false, that Pénélope was the one? He had asked her: Was what we had not good enough? Did it not feel right? What of our years together?

There may be another love, another woman, another betrayal even, waiting—but what of his decision to love Pénélope to the end, whereby he'd partitioned his soul?

All paths led back to her.

"How did this happen?" he'd asked Pénélope. Words he had spoken to her that were now irrelevant came to his mind, like pieces cut from different puzzles—*enough*, *right*, *years*.

She had looked at him as if to say: *Falling in love is not a road that can be retraced; it is an end that hides its own origins, a path in deep winter whose tracks fill with snow.*

Certain words were permanently ruined for him, words that stretched longer in his memory than Pénélope's speaking of them: *intense, connection, ever*. Those three words strung together, with her intonation—she was trying not to hurt him and had come up with this?—her beautiful small wrists, her emphasis on *ever felt*: taken together, these words were the final sally of a round of bullets.

Some days, his love for Pénélope stood like an impediment before him. It was monstrous, and whole, and impossible to grasp all at once; he could touch it only as a guide, his left arm extended as if feeling his way out of a maze, know it in pieces as he tried to lead himself out.

XVIII

In the car, the two sisters sat silently. They were west of the borough of Saint-Laurent, on Côte-de-Liesse, when Pénélope turned toward Lille and said: "I don't know what it is about him. I was so cruel, I threw it in his face." Lille touched her sister's knee. "It's always like that," she said. "There's no way around it. C'était une rupture."

The next morning, though, it was as if the last three years had never happened. Pénélope thought: This skirt I wear is the only skirt, this red-and-yellow scarf the only scarf. I will take the only road into the only city to meet my only love. I am carrying his child.

She felt her body, a pillar, blunt the autumn wind; she stood like a still fortress in the dawning light. Gabriel, she knew, would already be at the top of Mount Royal, waiting for her.

Life yawned and stretched in her thirty-year-old body.

Five days later, they got married. Pénélope had called her father to invite him to the civil ceremony at the courthouse on Notre-Dame. She then called Lille, who arrived early the day of the wedding to help her sister with her hair. Gabriel's mother, on three days' notice, took time off work and drove the two hours from Oka.

There are two photographs from their wedding day. In one, Pénélope is wearing a knee-length sequinned white dress from Zara. Gabriel stands next to her, his fingers in the crook of her arm. Lille is open-mouthed, speaking to her brother-in-law, her left hand in the air. In the other, Gabriel and his father-in-law are shaking hands, Pénélope's father mid-laugh.

Beyond the marriage itself, Pénélope and Gabriel were delighted that their hidden affair was now out in the open: that Pénélope could take the two keys she always had to conceal in her purse, one gold and one silver, and place them on her key ring, a partner's privilege; that Gabriel could set that photograph of her, taken one morning as she looked out the window, her blouse partially unbuttoned, on his desk at work.

They decided on Cuba, finally, for their honeymoon. The room they rented was at the back of an old house in Central Havana, separated from the rest of the bed and breakfast by a dark green, heavy-smelling garden. There was a kitchen too hot and enclosed to cook in, an open-air shower, and their bedroom, the long side of the double bed pushed against a wall, the room lit with a soft yellow bulb, a dark red rug on the floor in front of an antennaed television set. They had tried to be quiet, their first few nights there, but eventually they surrendered, two people digging deeply and blindly into shared earth.

Walking down the streets of Havana, they bought bottles of soda water—with a touch of rum, for Gabriel—and sat along the Malecón, turning to face the ocean and then swivelling back at the sound of a guitar, the prompting of a singer.

On the beach they had chosen as theirs, the one they discovered by randomly stepping off the public bus that shuttled down the coast, they started to discuss baby names.

"Arielle," said Pénélope.

Gabriel shook his head. "Kristin," he offered.

"No, you see," Pénélope said, her still-wet, sand-covered foot resting atop his ankle, her leg alongside his. "We have to find a name that works in both French and English."

"Stéphanie," said Gabriel.

"That was Adrien's ex-girlfriend's name," said Pénélope. "Veto."

"Veto," Gabriel said. "Véto. That works."

"That does not work," Pénélope laughed, kicking the soft, cool sand against his shins.

And, even there, she could tell Gabriel was distracted. It was as if a part of him were still missing to her, like a page she'd skipped over in her reading of him that she couldn't go back to. As if he had a secret that had been made easier to conceal by all the other secrets they had kept, all the lies they had told, and was now suddenly evident, a tiny corner of him pulled away at every moment.

Pénélope, weeks later, would realize she had no lasting impressions of Havana at all; all she could remember was the nights in bed, and their walks through the city, her focus on his stride, on his body not a foot from hers, the slight pressure of his hand in her own.

Back in Montreal, they started to speak about their future, now laden with guarantees: of keeping Pénélope's car, an old Volkswagen Beetle from the 1990s, currently stored in the backyard of the house left to the daughters by their late mother; of holding on to that house, in case their own daughter one day decided to go to McGill; of where they would spend their anniversary, their years of good health, of how each of them would be, at sixty, at eighty, at a hundred.

XIX

Kill him, Gabriel finally decided, placing the bag of cut corn and smoked turkey Pénélope handed him in the trunk of the car. Kill him before my child is born.

From the other side of the table Pénélope looked formidable, like an earth goddess, a growling lioness.

"And you would leave me here, six months' pregnant."

"Pen, I still wake up wanting to kill him," Gabriel said. "I want to find out what happened, find out the truth. I want this to be over before Chloe is born."

Pénélope didn't answer. She looked to the waitress clearing plates at the next table. Behind Gabriel, a man and his daughter were playing chess; in the silence between them she could hear the slamming of bishops and knights into wooden time clocks.

"You do realize," she said slowly, "that what you're doing is no different. That our daughter, like you, will grow up fatherless."

"Sweetheart," Gabriel started. As soon as he'd said it, they both knew it was the first hollow word that had ever passed between them. Reaching over for her hand in apology, he continued. "I'm coming back, you know. As soon as I find him."

"What if he's already left North Bay?"

The day before, Gabriel had gotten a call from his godmother, a nurse at the hospital in North Bay. I think he's here, she had said. I'm not sure. I haven't told your mother.

"I know. I'm afraid of that, too," Gabriel said.

Pénélope closed her eyes. There it was again, that note in his voice; that same ache she'd heard when he first told her his mother's story. His voice a taut, pulled string. She reached across the table with her other hand, resting her fingers against his elbow and caressing the length of his arm.

"When would you need to leave?" she asked.

"Tomorrow," he replied.

Pénélope made up her mind. She decided to let her life fall into step with his; she would hold his hand and climb aboard his train, even as she felt it barrel down a lost and ruined track.

The air in the bedroom was dense and close. Pénélope stood on her tiptoes, Gabriel's arms around her; her pregnant belly between them, his shoulder bag pressed awkwardly into her waist, she felt cocooned, safe.

She watched as Gabriel lifted his bag off of the bed and carried it toward the door. She felt their love as if she had slid her fingers into the one firm handhold on a slippery cliff.

If someone had told her then, *this will be the last time you see him*, she would not have believed them; she would not have believed that their love was also mortal.

XX

When Adrien next saw Pénélope, she was walking down Saint Denis, her belly large even through her heavy winter coat. She was carrying four bulky shopping bags.

"Pénélope," he called.

She turned; for a brief second he saw how she would glance at a stranger. Then she waved, and Adrien strode rapidly across the street toward her. He had been on his way to the Sainte-Élisabeth for a beer with Sébastien, and now knew that he would be late—but he knew his old friend would forgive him this, too.

They had walked half a block down Saint Denis and were almost at de Maisonneuve when Adrien stopped in front of a chocolaterie.

"Remember this place?"

"Of course." Pénélope smiled. She felt like a bowstring, loosened and set to rest for the night; gentle.

"Shall we order some hot chocolate?" he asked.

XXI

Gabriel felt suddenly lost, as if he hadn't grown up in North Bay. He took a taxi to the hospital from the bus station. Using a different entrance from the one he remembered from his childhood—he had spent hours here whenever Lucas had been paged on the drive back from school, in the years the doctor and his mother had been together—he approached the receptionist's desk, explained who he was, and asked to see Dr. Harrison.

"It's been a long time," Gabriel said. His voice was raspy, deep; the way it sounded in early morning. He realized, standing in front of the doctor—this man who had delivered him, proposed to his mother four times, and who, the fourth time she had said no, had driven her to Oka himself to help set up her new life—that he hadn't spoken a word to anyone since he'd left Montreal.

"I'm looking for a man," Gabriel continued, clearing his throat, stepping through the open door of the office. "I need to know if he's still in the hospital. A friend of mine called a few days ago to let me know he was here."

Lucas nodded. He had checked the patient's drowsy pupils himself, watched his surgeon's hands tremble as he reached for the chart; realizing who the man was, he'd marched out of the emergency room, leaden anger spreading through his body, down to his feet, into his fingertips. Fifteen minutes later, Lucas had strode back into the emergency room with a vial of potassium chloride, only to find that Marcel Tremblay had left against medical advice.

"So he's been here."

"He was here three days ago," he said quietly.

Lucas led Gabriel out of his office and down a well-lit hall into a dark room. He closed the door behind them and turned on the light.

"You'll find what you need in here." He paused. "The chart is labelled with the first three letters of his last name. I'll stand guard outside the door for five minutes."

Lucas looked at Gabriel, and thought: He has his father's eyes.

The file, when Gabriel found it, contained little. On the carbon-copied patient admittance forms his father had left no permanent address, no registered phone number, and no employment information. His local address was a Comfort Inn. Gabriel turned to leave—wary of the metronomic click of heels down the spare hallway—and was about to slide the brown folder back into place, when he found it: the all-important photocopy paper-clipped to the back page.

Gabriel's knowledge of his father doubled. From the OHIP card he discovered that Marcel Tremblay was actually Marcel René Tremblay, born January 24, 1946. There was a blurry photograph. A signature. And there, on the back, a government-endorsed address in Ottawa.

Gabriel had done everything he could think of. After going to the motel, and then taking the bus to Ottawa—a five-hour journey that had brought him to a locked apartment door and to a mailbox stuffed full of another man's bills—he had gone north, and then west, back toward North Bay.

For three weeks he peddled his father's grainy, blown-up photograph to every convenience store, gas station, and motel in the vicinity. He wandered up and down the boardwalk near Lake Nipissing, thrusting the picture into strangers' faces. He knew that, soon, he himself would be recognized; that within a matter of days he would run into someone from his old life, someone who would call his mother hundreds of kilometres away in Oka. He knew that she would discover, finally, what he had spent thirty-four years trying to hide from her: that the chain that slowed her steps—and had kept her from being able to commit to Lucas, the man she loved—bound him, too.

Afterwards, he hitchhiked from North Bay back to Ottawa, stopping in every town and hamlet on the way, wielding his father's photograph, the vial of potassium chloride with its needle and syringe pushed to the bottom of his rucksack.

Another month passed. Around him, the northern boulders lay huddled and sleeping under a thick mantle of heavy snow. Lake Nipissing was frozen, the crack of its ice like thunder in the evenings, its back veined with the criss-cross of snowmobiles, of moose tracks.

He rented a car. When he'd called Pénélope at home for their insurance information, she had asked, coldly, almost uninterestedly, if he had found his father yet.

Almost, he told her. Tomorrow, he said to himself.

Driving through stone-flat fields, past lovers' names etched large on highway rock, he felt the dried yellow grains of his old life turn and rush, headlong, into the smooth white sands of the new.

He retraced the familiar curves of the road like a man leading himself out of a maze, out of a forest with a trail of bread crumbs.

At first, the Internet searches using his father's full name had turned up hundreds of seemingly useful results. Gabriel had, for example, immediately found an old interview in the *Kingston Whig-Standard* online archives that quoted his father's name directly:

> The volunteering program, founded in 1972 by prison guards Lise Desvallées and Marcel Tremblay, pairs local teenagers from Notre Dame Catholic High School and Queen's University with inmates eager to complete their high-school education. "Over the last five years, we've had hundreds of inmates satisfy the requirements for a high school diploma, thanks to these kids," said Desvallées. "Education is such an important part of the rehabilitation we do here."

Gabriel had tried to find Lise Desvallées. He had driven all the way to her hometown of Medway, Maine, only to discover, seated in the microfilm room at the small public library, that she had died from cancer a few years earlier.

After this, the location of his father, as gleaned from Google, became more far-fetched. What were the chances, after all, that his father, so recently in North Bay, now operated a fly-fishing outfit on the Bow River? That he was on the guest list at a high-end nightclub in Vancouver? Still, certain only of his desire to see each lead wound down to the ends of its thread, Gabriel turned south, onto the I-95, and then west, toward Calgary.

On the way to Alberta, he called Pénélope. Recently, driving in increasingly erratic triangles—from North Bay to Ottawa, from Ottawa to North Bay, into northeastern Maine via Ottawa again, and now heading west, at least as far as Calgary, all the while moving, ostensibly, in tighter and tighter circles around his target, closing in on him like a noose—he found that his life had unwound itself from hers almost completely. He knew nothing about her day-to-day life: whether or not she had slept well the night before, which of her clothes still fit, what colour she'd painted the nursery.

So, slowly, he left Pénélope behind. It felt as if a ghost were marching him down a prisoner's path, with shackles and chains around his feet—a single-file path marked for him alone.

When Gabriel reached Calgary, he pulled over on the side of the road and fell asleep, two blocks from the hotel he had booked online earlier that day. He was so tired he couldn't follow the directions of the GPS, turning left on Glenmore Trail instead of right, and then missing the turnoff for Blackfoot Trail completely.

He felt drained from the non-stop drive from Saskatoon; this, combined with the exhaustion of having to look every single man he met directly in the face.

The last place Gabriel went before heading on foot into the Laurentians, only days before the thread guiding him out of the maze stretched and broke:

The prison stood before him like a fortress. This time, on the phone with the chief corrections officer, he had told the truth: that his father, Marcel Tremblay, had been employed there; that, after 1975, the man had disappeared without a trace; that Marcel Tremblay would soon have a granddaughter, and finding him was a matter of life and death.

Gabriel was met at the front gate by a woman in her late thirties. She'd already said she wouldn't be able to help, that Marcel's file had been closed years ago and was stored away in a dusty Ottawa office, that the penitentiary itself had lost track of him in 1974. Still, Gabriel asked to be let in—to see the officers' stations, the empty cells, the grounds, the library—if only to be where his father had been, to know where to go next.

What Gabriel left out: that, sometime in the last three months, the desire to kill his father had turned out to be nothing more than a desire to know him.

XXII

An entire season had passed with no word. Pénélope had felt the baby kick; while shopping for maternity clothes, her water had broken all over the terrazzo floor of the Bay. It had been her sister, finally, who had accompanied her to the Royal Vic. During the delivery, between her contractions, she had turned her face to the wall.

Pénélope sat completely still. Her shoes were untied, the black laces springing up like the unsewn stitches of a wound. For the last hour, she had found herself incapable of bending down and tightening them, and therefore unable to stride out the door, walk down the stairs, and buy fruit from Atwater Market.

Chloe lay sleeping in the next room. Pénélope willed her to wake up, to cry, to force Pénélope to stand, walk over to her.

How to escape the days she spent half-asleep and the nights she lay half-awake, the four hours it took to eat any meal, the moans through the wall that woke Chloe, the long afternoons of tears that left her curled like a dried husk on the tiled floor?

And then, finally, a month after his daughter's birth, Gabriel made an early-morning long-distance phone call to Montreal. He heard Pénélope's tired voice, followed by silence when she realized it was him.

"This isn't worth it," he said. "If I don't find him in the next day—in the next twenty-four hours—I promise I'll come home."

Pénélope remained quiet. In the distance, behind her, he heard the scrape of morning street cleaners on Saint Augustin. Then her attempt at words: her voice high-pitched, her breath jagged. Over her, he said, "I'm coming now, right now, I'll be there by tonight, I completely fucked this up, I'm such a fool."

Pénélope hung up.

XXIII

When his fingertips brushed hers on the train paused at
Lionel-Groulx, on a warm August afternoon four years
after they had first met, Araceli looked up at the tall man
who had touched her, and for a second did not recognize
Adrien's widely spaced eyes, his earnest face.

Together, they strolled by the canal. When Araceli men-
tioned that she'd just moved back from New York into an
apartment nearby, and that she didn't have any evening
plans, they walked to Atwater Market and bought steaks
and asparagus to grill for dinner.

"Well, I did leave because of you," Araceli said. "I just
didn't want you to know. I didn't want you to feel bad.
And you shouldn't, because New York turned out to be
great for me."

"I'm so sorry," Adrien said. "I don't remember the details,
but I don't think I handled that well."

Araceli didn't reply, but laced her arm through his, so
that they continued on arm in arm.

Adrien told her of his break-up with Pénélope, the child
that wasn't his, about running into Pénélope months later.

"She was in good spirits. I think she was five or six months'
pregnant at the time, and her husband, the guy she had left
me for, had just left on a big trip," he said. "I ran into her
again after their daughter Chloe was born. Her husband
still wasn't back yet."

Adrien described walking Pénélope home, and then
helping her carry her stroller up the stairs.

"And then, to see her apartment," he said slowly. "Clothes
everywhere. A slipper here, a slipper there. Dried chicken
bones on a plate, left on the floor. Envelopes piled up
outside the door."

He told Araceli how, after that, he had started to stop by
every week, to check on her.

"I think I will always want to help her," he said. Adrien thought back to his partitioned soul, to the broken remnants of a love he hadn't known what to do with, and to his eventual solution: to care for her without being in love with her, to allow himself to love someone else.

That night, having talked and laughed for hours, they fell asleep together, inches apart, in Araceli's new bed.

XXIV

I miss you—the words were powerful now, now that they had been said once, and meant once. Pénélope would never be able to use them again, having heard Gabriel say them to her; to do so would be to spit on an unguarded memory, on the flesh of a shivering white mollusk, vulnerable out of its shell.

She wanted to punish him by speaking smoothly to him. To throw his way the lake, unrippled, with a staring moon. No more the waves, dark, heavy, rough, battering; the deep blind fish, swimming slowly. To slide across to him like ice.

Pénélope thought: I want to turn you into a relic, a brown god, enclosed roughly in rocks, bowed down to; I want to see you in an alcove above me, another's limbs tied into mine.

Oh, to enter the earth as if born on this day. To arrive before old loves darken the sunrise, before the heavy tread sinks into one's heels.

To have avoided, forever and eternally, that night in April, Gabriel's dark eyes lingering against hers, her bare knee touching his as the bistro dimmed the lights, closed the shutters. To have avoided standing beside him, the closeness of his body as he waited, his arm extended, for a car in the night rain; the soft wool cuffs of his trousers already wet.

She would scheme, to make it seem like she'd died; she would have a child with another man, so that the blend of their features would haunt Gabriel.

Pénélope thought: Oh, to be able to say, as a family at an airline check-in counter, "Yes, we packed the bag ourselves," and hold our daughter by the hand.

Pénélope prayed for time to run out. She prayed for it to drop out from under her, like a trap door. To bring her to where she could lie, still on cold wooden boards, a coarse cloth over her face like a shroud.

Oh, she wanted to tear out her love.

But it had sunk through her now. It was lead, and like lead tied to one's ankles, it pulled her down.

The memory of that afternoon in Havana: a bird scratching the windowsill, his hands under her billowing white blouse, his eyes open as if a dam had broken.

It will sink, sink, sink.

XXV

In a way, Gabriel had known it would come to this—to ground warfare, hand-to-hand combat, a scorching of the earth. The small blue rental Corolla was parked kilometres away from where Gabriel now stood in the forest, his arms by his sides, a gruff, two-day-old beard on his jaw and neck. Gabriel had seen this path in his dreams—had stumbled down it, his hands stretched out in front of him, as if blind; now he followed his father's footsteps, the shoe prints frozen into the hardened mud.

He was exhausted. For two days he had cracked the ice skin of morning puddles with his sharp heel, kneeling to dip first his ear, then his stubbled cheek, and then the corner of his mouth into the murky water. He had eaten only a crumbling Hershey's bar.

And then Marcel's tracks completely disappeared, but this didn't surprise Gabriel. In the last few hours he had started to wonder: the ranger who had crinkled his old eyes over his father's photograph and then pointed to the path into the hills—what did he know? The large, rugged footsteps Gabriel had been following, literally placing his own feet in them as he walked—whose were they? Did they really belong to Marcel Tremblay? Was Marcel Tremblay really his father? And, of the hundreds of Marcel Tremblays born in Canada over the last fifty years, how could he be sure he'd ever been chasing the right one?

And then, the biggest question of all: when you and your life's happiness part ways at a forked path, when do you admit the mistake and turn back, and when do you set yourself belligerently forward?

Gabriel turned around. He set his brave feet along the sunnier path. The white sands rushed back into the other half of the hourglass, but it was already too late. Gabriel, unaware, walked briskly over spring shoots and small shrubs, imagining himself in Montreal by midnight.

A few hours later, having emerged from the forest onto the highway that would take him home—but first, on a walk a few kilometres south, to where he had parked the Corolla—Gabriel failed to see the pickup truck as it rounded the corner and sped toward him.

The driver, too, failed to see Gabriel, concealed in dusk's half-light, in muddied clothing, in this completely unexpected place. The seconds slowed; Gabriel felt time yawn open to accommodate every possible avenue of escape, but the ditch was too far, and the truck too fast, for him to leap aside or to jump.

In the instant before the grille of the truck bore into the bones of his legs, the flesh of his torso, in the moment before he pushed through the eye of the needle, time gave him one last gift: he saw in a flash Chloe, as a woman—a lanky girl with long slender legs, a swan's neck, and her mother's bright, ingenuous eyes. And as the truck crushed his knees, he felt his love for her like a deep inhale with no end.

XXVI

Every evening, swinging a crying Chloe near her crib, Pénélope contemplated a different set of knives. How, now, to open every suffered wound on his body?

And how to punish Gabriel for leaving her when he still loved her: how to take revenge for that?

Pénélope never thought to check the obituaries in the *Montreal Gazette*. She had thought of everything else: she had attended every neighbourhood party, wineglass in hand, to catch any echo of his name tied to another's; she had walked by his ex-girlfriend Caroline's window; she had even called Gabriel's uncle, whom she had never met, who didn't even know she existed.

Pénélope had no way of knowing that Gabriel was dead. She didn't know that the driver of the pickup truck had backed up, swerved in a wild arc around Pénélope's husband's crumpled form, and then stopped ten kilometres down the road to vomit. She didn't know that it had taken forty-five minutes for Gabriel to actually die, and another five hours for a patrol car to find him. She didn't know about the abandoned rental car that had eventually been stolen, or that his wallet still lay where it had fallen out of his pocket among the moss-covered stones on a forest path. She had missed the three-inch article, "Man Killed Near Saint-Sauveur," because love cannot accept anything as impartial as death; in his disappearance, Pénélope could only read betrayal.

A plan unfolded. It was utterly unforgivable; it was perfect; it would set the future as a bleak, charred expanse between them.

"I actually considered ringing the doorbell and just leaving her on the doorstep," Pénélope said wryly, as Adrien opened the door. "Maybe with a note. You would have loved that."

Adrien smiled as he reached for Chloe. The baby kicked her legs happily against his familiar ribs.

"Do you need me to keep her for a few days?"

"It might be more than a few," Pénélope said lightly.

Adrien looked up. Pénélope seemed taller, thinner; her deep brown eyes had sunk into her face. She looked as if a warm wind could blow her off the face of the earth.

Adrien reached out and touched her cheek. Pénélope bent her face toward his hand. He was allowed this small affection, now; now that he had Araceli upstairs, recently moved-in, her books alongside his books, the weight of her head on his chest in the mornings.

"He's not back yet."

"No."

Adrien held the baby tightly against his shoulder.

"Chloe can stay here as long as you need."

Adrien had no way of knowing that three weeks would turn into three years, into thirteen years, into a lifetime of shielding his adopted daughter from the truth—that he had half-expected the phone call that came two weeks later, the notification of the next of kin. That he was unsurprised when the consular official told him, in her bad-news tone, of Pénélope's drowning off Cuba's coast, of the six scuba-tour witnesses, of the group leader who swore up and down that he had seen her dark head sink beneath the rough waves of the sea.

Pénélope acted quickly. She called and left a message for Amélie, her oldest friend and only accomplice; she walked east on Saint Catherine toward Saint Denis and paid for her fake passport; she booked a room at a Sainte-Julienne hotel under this new, false name. She withdrew four thousand dollars from her savings account at TD, mentioning loudly to the teller how warm it was going to be in Cuba.

Online, she booked a return flight from Montreal to Havana in her own name, leaving the next day and returning in three weeks. She wouldn't, of course, ever use the second ticket; it would be lying innocently on top of her holiday wear when embassy and insurance officials, accompanied by the Cuban police, packed up her things and repatriated them.

Gabriel would remember that he loved her, when he found out she was dead. And when he put two and two together—when he realized that she was alive, and that her crime against him matched his crime against her—he would never want to see her again.

And: if her death was now the only way to remind Gabriel of his love for her, it was, ironically, also the only way she could bring him home.

On the plane, she missed her daughter; the soft weight of her flesh in her lap.

And so it was that Pénélope heard the soft, pattering footsteps of death not once, but twice: first under stormy Cuban waves, and then again a month later, when she plummeted like deadweight into the St. Lawrence River.

The first time, she had escaped. She had seduced the gallant, handsome scuba-diving instructor at the all-inclusive resort with the story of an abusive husband, and he, Julián, had arranged the rest.

On the day of the fateful dive, Julián had fitted her personally. After adjusting her weight belt, puffing up her vest, and checking her regulator and pressure gauges, he slipped a compass into her wet hands.

"Go east," he had whispered. "My brother will be waiting for you."

The blue waves were choppy against the rusting motorboat as they left Havana. They had intentionally chosen a tempestuous day. Diving last, Pénélope reached the bottom, waited for Julián to lead the others toward the reef and then swam, hard, to the east. Martín, waiting two hundred metres away in the murky, hidden seas, had brought the extra air tank they would need to share; an hour later, having traversed a kilometre of ocean and sweating under her wetsuit, Pénélope boarded a motorboat back to Havana.

Later that night, in the brothers' kitchen, she coloured her hair blond with leftover dye Martín's girlfriend had left under the sink. Then, using the fake passport that had cost twice as much as her flight home, she landed in Montreal the very moment the dismayed rescue workers called off their search.

The second time, of course, wasn't so simple.

She imagined Gabriel's first thought, upon hearing the news of her death: of her being pulled into the current, under the waves, her pale skin nibbled and gnawed by a hundred small fish.

Amélie sat across from her, dressed in black: a matching patterned skirt, silk blouse, and heels. Pénélope, on the other hotel bed, watched her friend with newly green eyes.

"Thank you for these," she said quietly.

Amélie nodded. Pénélope got up and put the other six pairs of contact lenses in the mini-fridge and then sat back down on the bed.

"I'm sorry, Amélie."

"I don't think that's enough," she said. "You have no idea how devastated people are. You're just sitting in here dreaming up vengeance for your stupid affair. And I helped you. I made this happen."

"Amélie."

"No," Amélie said. She stood up and began pacing the faded beige carpet. She opened the window—pulling it upward, hard, giving a small cry as it came unstuck—and, noticing a couple walk by on the street outside, immediately lowered her voice.

"Did you know that Ian Matthews came to the funeral? I haven't seen him since high school. Dozens of people came, Pénélope."

"Amélie," Pénélope said. "Was he there?"

Amélie sat down again. The warm, early-September breeze blew loose strands of hair against her cheek. She looked down at her perfectly polished shoes.

"You know, I don't think I really believed, until right now, that you'd done all of this for him," she said. "I was sure there had to be some other reason."

"Amélie. Just tell me."

Amélie's thin mouth pressed into a straight line. She stood, moving to sit beside Pénélope. She wrapped both arms around her friend's waist and rested her head on Pénélope's shoulder.

"No," Amélie whispered. "I looked everywhere. He wasn't there."

Pénélope didn't respond.

"Adrien was there. And you should have seen Chloe. She had no idea what was going on."

"Stop," Pénélope said.

The secret Pénélope died with:

That—after hiding on the outskirts of Montreal for three weeks, hiring a man to photograph the signatures in the register at her own funeral, and discovering that Gabriel really hadn't attended, or called, or even gone by the apartment to look for Chloe—she felt her love for him start to fall from her shoulders like a snake's moulting skin.

That—after seeing the photographs and videos brought to her by Amélie, and watching her grandfather, his wrinkled hand and bent arm brought to his face to hide his tears—she'd felt so mortified she really had wanted to die.

Intolerable to her was the certainty that her love would regenerate, that her heart would nose out a different skin. That someone else could come to mean as much to her. That her memory of the night she had lain beside Gabriel—rain pouring down the windows, moonlight on his naked face, the tender words she had whispered that she knew he wouldn't hear—would become placid, fond, maybe forgotten entirely.

And, now that she felt but the fading tendrils of love for him, how to reconcile what she had done to the ones who had, in the end, cared more? Every morning for months she had felt Gabriel's betrayal like a boulder set on her sternum, unable to draw a full breath into her lungs. It had kept her in bed as Chloe cried, for minutes, and once, for hours, until the baby, exhausted and hungry, had fallen back asleep. To live out her days with this new sinking weight, her guilt to replace his betrayal?

How to go on, and know: that her love for Gabriel, and his having left her, had meant more to her than Chloe?

No—before that the bridge; before that the half-ice and rocks below.

Nobody walks along this bridge. There is a long, lonely footpath that stretches all the way to Longueuil, but today it was deserted, as Pénélope knew it would be. This death—the real one—will be sharp as an icy guillotine; the St. Lawrence will slide through her muscle and bone like the edge of a knife.

The steel rafters thrummed wildly under her fingertips. A cold autumn wind whipped her hair around her face as she pulled off her shoes and set them under the bench, next to her gloves. Using her toes to climb up the metal grille, Pénélope paused, poised on the thick iron railing, as balanced and relaxed as a dancer. The river below her was flush with grey rain and early ice. Pénélope recalled scampering onto the balustrade of the lookout point in North Hatley, decades ago, with Lille. She smiled. For the first time in weeks, she thought of stepping down.

Before she jumped, before the animal panic of a tumbling body overcame coherent thought, Pénélope felt a note of triumph: One day, Gabriel, you will look up from your work and suddenly remember me, she thought. And I will be gone.

And while she fell: The slope of your neck into your shoulders; what had made my heart ache now has the consistency of dried pebbles in my hand.

INVISIBLE PUBLISHING produces fine Canadian literature for those who enjoy such things. As a not-for-profit publisher, our work includes building communities that sustain and encourage engaging, literary, and current writing.

Invisible Publishing has been in operation for over a decade. We released our first fiction titles in the spring of 2007, and our catalogue has come to include works of graphic fiction and non-fiction, pop culture biographies, experimental poetry, and prose.

We are committed to publishing diverse voices and experiences. In acknowledging historical and systemic barriers, and the limits of our existing catalogue, we strongly encourage LGBTQ2SIA+, Indigenous, and writers of colour to submit their work.

Invisible Publishing is also home to the Bibliophonic series of music books and the Throwback series of CanLit reissues.

If you'd like to know more, please get in touch:
info@invisiblepublishing.com